What They're §

'Disappearing Diamor
young readers.' *The W*

'Move over McGruff the Crime Dog, Upton Charles is here to sniff for clues and solve your mysteries.' *Cantabrigia*

'This dog takes a bite out of crime.' *Cambridge Chronicle*

'Perfect for the read-to-me or the I-can-read-it myself age group.' *Boston Globe*

'D. G. Stern's delightful series of adventures starring Upton Charles.' *Flipkart.com*

'Upton Charles will make a believer out of every reader.' *Midwest Book Review*

'To solve the paw-fect crime, call Upton!' *The Harvard Coop*

'Told from the viewpoint of a very special dog, "Winter Wonderland" promises to be a great mystery reading experience for kids ages 8-11. "Winter Wonderland" also can be read aloud by an adult as an exciting chapter book for a younger audience.' *Midwest Book Review*

'The action-packed mysteries are intended to be "read with me" books so that parents and teachers can be involved with reading at an earlier age. Older readers can also read through and enjoy them on their own.' *NewportPatch*

'Logical deductive thinking, teamwork, paying attention to random clues to put the jigsaw puzzle together, who would think these skills could be helped and taught by a dog, even a very smart dog?' *Entrepreneur.com*

'As a teacher of constructive logical, deductive thought, Upton rules.' *Midwest Book Review*

UPTON CHARLES

Dog Detective

Disappearing Diamonds

By D.G. Stern

Illustrations by Deborah Allison

NEPTUNE PRESS

WWW.NEPTUNEPRESS.ORG

NEPTUNE PRESS

WWW.UPTONCHARLES.COM

Printed in the U.S.A.

Publisher's Cataloging-In-Publication Data

Stern, D. G.
  Upton Charles, dog detective. Disappearing diamonds / by D.G. Stern ; illustrations by Deborah Allison.

  pages : illustrations ; cm

  Summary: Upton is a little white Bichon Frise dog who loves to dig for clues. This time our dog detective is recruited to help find the Van Camp diamonds that have disappeared from the local museum. Join Upton as he sniffs out evidence to find a valuable missing necklace.
  First issued 2010 with same ISBN; reissued 2014 with new illustrator, copyright date, and LCCN.
  Interest age level: 008-011.
  ISBN: 978-0-9828098-4-6

  1. Dogs--Juvenile fiction. 2. Bichon frise--Juvenile fiction. 3. Diamond jewelry--Juvenile fiction. 4. Jewelry theft--Juvenile fiction. 5. Dogs--Fiction. 6. Jewelry--Fiction. 7. Diamonds--Fiction. 8. Mystery and detective stories. 9. Mystery fiction. I. Allison, Deborah, 1967- II. Title. III. Title: Disappearing diamonds

PZ7.S74 Upd 2014
[Fic]   2013922985

They say that diamonds are a girl's best friend.
But a dog is always man's best friend.

CHAPTER ONE
Morning at the Charles House

"Upton...shhh," Dad mumbles.

Good morning, Charles family! It's getting late. Maybe I'll whine again.

"Upton, it's 5:30 in the morning, and it's Saturday. Be quiet. Go back to sleep."

Uh oh, I'm in big trouble now. I better learn to tell time. It's not fair. The sun is coming up, which means everyone should be getting up. What do I care what the dumb old clock says, anyway? I can see the sun. I know it's Saturday, and everyone wants to sleep in, but I need to arrange my play date with Phoebe. The anticipation is killing me. I probably should try to go back to sleep. Yes, I'll do just that. Even though I am not very big, I can jump extraordinarily well. And I do...right onto Mom and Dad's big bed. I search for a nice spot to lie in.

"Upton," Mom mutters. "Why are you lying on top of me?"

Before she can move me or get real angry, I decide to give her a kiss, a doggy kiss. I lick her ear. She makes a funny sound. Then she goes back to sleep.

I've really got to figure out how to tell time. How hard can it be? Maybe when I am four. It can't be that difficult, can it?

What's that sound? It must be the twins downstairs watching TV. It's pretty loud. I'm awake now. I think I'll join them. Maybe they will take me out for a walk or over to Phoebe's. Everyone says that we are so cute together. Cute? Who cares? She's my best friend and we like to play. Cute? Sometimes big people say things that really don't make sense. But you already know that. I'll be satisfied if the twins just give me breakfast. I'm starving.

I jump off the bed as quietly as I can and run downstairs. Veronica and Alex are eating something that smells very good while they watch TV. I really don't understand the big deal about TV. You sit in front of a box all day when you should be playing.

Oh! I forgot to tell you! My name is Upton

Charles. I am a Bichon Frise (that's "BEE-shon free-ZEY"), a little white dog, and so is Phoebe. I live in a big yellow house. Well, it seems big to me, but remember, I am only three. Anyway, I live with Veronica and Alex. Some people call them Ronny and Al, but they don't like those names because it makes them both sound like boys. They are twins, but they don't look exactly the same. I can tell them apart. They don't smell the same. All you humans have a unique smell to us dogs. And besides, Veronica is a girl and Alex is a boy.

The twins are eleven years old and are in the fifth grade. They play with me a lot. Veronica and Alex are very careful when we play together, and they never hit me or throw things at me. On occasion they will throw things at each other and get into fights. It's very funny watching them try to kick each other, unless of course one of them gets hurt. Then Mom gets real mad. The twins are beginning to figure out that when Mom gets mad, very bad things happen...like no TV or no friends.

A few weeks ago, Phoebe's parents had to go away on a trip, and she stayed at our house for a whole week. Awesome! All we did was play, eat, and sleep. Every once in a while, we'd go out for a walk. It was definitely cool.

"Hi, Upton," Alex greets me. "Do you want to go out?"

Of course I want to go out, but I also want a taste of whatever you are eating. It certainly looks good. Something with frosting on it. I shouldn't eat too much sweet stuff, but neither should the twins.

"Do you want a piece of donut?" Veronica asks.

Thanks, sounds great to me. "Sit down!"

Okay, I'll sit down if it means I'll get a treat. Veronica hands me a small piece of her chocolate donut.

"Veronica, don't give him chocolate," Alex shouts. "He's not supposed to eat it."

Alex is right. Dogs aren't supposed to eat chocolate, but the piece is small.

"It's just a little piece." Veronica scratches my ear.

"Okay, but don't give him any more. I'll check his dish and make sure it's filled."

Ugh! That means no more donut, just dog food and water. People are always wondering why dogs beg at the table for human food. Try to eat dog food some day. Think about it, would you rather have water and dog food or steak and milk? Be real. I wonder what we are going to do today.

Veronica and Alex will probably sit and watch TV until Dad turns it off and says something like, 'Let's go, couch potatoes.' I am not sure what that means, but the twins move when he says it. I hope Mom and Dad wake up soon. It'd be totally awesome if they make a big breakfast. I always get a bite or two...or three. And then we can go out, do some doggy things and maybe go down to the beach so I can chase seagulls. What would I do if I ever caught one? Yuck!

CHAPTER TWO
The Diamonds are Missing!

I guess the twins are having a good time. They are laughing and eating donuts, but they won't give me any more. Good news. I hear Dad coming down the stairs. That means breakfast cannot be far behind.

"Hey, couch potatoes, do you want Dad's special French toast for breakfast?"

"Yes, awesome."

Veronica's mouth is full of the rest of her donut, but she still wants more food...just like me.

"Thanks, Dad," adds Alex, trying to sound more grown-up than his sister.

I just wag my tail. But I don't think anyone is paying attention to me. Hey, Dad, I want some, too. Dad's French toast with a little maple syrup is a perfect breakfast. I have learned in my three years of being on planet Earth that in order to get something around the Charles household, you have to make your wishes known. My answer to anything that concerns food is to sneeze. Yes... sneeze. Dogs aren't stupid, you know, especially a Bichon Frise with an appetite. I sneeze. Only twice. I don't want to appear too pushy.

"Okay, Upton, you can have some, too."

Dad is such a softy. The first thing Dad always does is to make coffee for Mom, and then the hot water for his tea. I am getting hungry. Please hurry up. Dad is a very organized cook. He puts everything he requires on the counter before beginning to mix things together.

Mom just starts to cook whenever she feels like it and puts things together as she goes along. She is an excellent cook, and everyone loves what she makes except...well, let me explain. Mom can't bake things like bread and cakes, because in order to bake, you need to follow directions, and Mom, well, she doesn't follow directions when she is cooking.

Dad gets the eggs, milk, bread, and bowl— everything he needs. Then he sets the table.

Hey, forget the table, just start cooking. I can't sit at the table anyway. Well, I actually could, but Mom would never allow me, especially during a meal. Being a dog sometimes has its drawbacks.

Just when I think Dad is ready to begin, he pours a large mug full of freshly brewed coffee and takes it upstairs to Mom. Okay, okay...no more interruptions, let's get serious. It's breakfast time. After what seems like an extremely long time, Dad finally returns to the kitchen and the preparation of breakfast finally begins. Soon, everything smells wonderful, and I notice that Dad is making a little bacon, too. I am very sensitive to smells, especially food.

"Kids, off with the television. Breakfast," he announces. The twins rush over to Dad, who hands them each a plate and a glass of orange juice.

My turn, my turn. Is anyone up there paying any attention to me? I sneeze.

"Okay, Upton, here's your French toast." And bacon? "And bacon." Dad puts a plate next to my dish. I don't get orange juice. That's okay, water is fine.

Okay, I'm done. Let's go out! Hello? Is anyone listening? Maybe if I sit real close to Dad, he'll give me some more from the table. Guess not. Mom is coming down the stairs. Well, that takes care of that. Mom will never let me eat from the table. I might as well give up and greet her. Hi, Mom! I wag my tail.

"Has anyone taken Upton out?" She asks.

No! I shout, but she cannot hear me. The twins shake their heads.

"No, he was just sitting with us, and he didn't go to the door or anything."

"If Upton's had an accident, both of you are going to clean it up."

Mom is serious, but I am insulted. I'm three, and I don't have accidents anymore.

"Would you like some French toast, dear?" Dad asks.

"No, thank you. I'll just sip my coffee on the porch while the dog goes out."

Mom opens the back door, and off I go into the yard. I do what I have to do and then start exploring to see if any more flowers have bloomed. Not yet. There is still too much snow on the ground, which I promptly roll in. It doesn't snow very often so I might as well take advantage of it.

"Upton, get out of the snow," Mom yells. "You'll get all wet and dirty."

Of course I'll get all wet and dirty. That's what playing is all about. Big people are so silly sometimes.

"Upton, come here and I'll dry you off," Dad calls.

Sounds good to me. Maybe I'll get a treat for being so cooperative. I sprint up the porch stairs, but suddenly Dad grabs me and briskly wipes off my paws with a towel.

"There you go, young man. No dirty paw prints on the furniture."

Dad can be so mean sometimes. The first thing I was going to do is run around the house with my wet paws and jump on all the chairs. Joke. Just kidding. Well, maybe kind of kidding...a little.

The phone rings. It is so disruptive. I

hate it, and it means that someone will be doing something other than playing with me. I can be so selfish, and hate is a very strong word.

Mom answers. "Hello, Charles residence. Hi, John, how are you? Of course, I'll get him. Oh, last night's opening was wonderful. You've got to be pleased. Absolutely everyone enjoyed themselves. Where did you get that band? It made me feel as if I was back in high school...and that was a very long time ago. Yes, here he is."

Mom puts her hand over the telephone receiver and says to Dad, "It's John Howard, and he seems upset. I can't imagine why. Last night was fabulous."

Dad shrugs his shoulders and takes the phone. "Hi John, what's up? Too big a mess to tidy up? I'm sure the museum took in enough money in donations to pay for a cleanup crew without having to ask Board members to grab a broom."

Dad is in a very cheerful mood, probably because of the French toast. But then he listens for a long time. "No way! When? I'll be over within an hour."

Dad hangs up the phone and slowly turns and says to Mom, "John told me that when he opened the museum this morning, he discovered that the Van Camp necklace is missing. There is no sign that anyone broke in. He said that he personally locked up after last night's event."

"Daddy, what's the Van Camp necklace?" the twins chime in together.

"Last night Mom and I went to a special party at the museum," Dad says.

"You guys were all dressed up," Veronica offers.

"That's right. There was a reception for the opening of a new show at the museum featuring pictures, costumes, paintings, and other things from what is called the Golden Age."

"You mean like old stuff?" Alex inserts.
"Yes, like the clothing and furniture wealthy people used in the late 1800s. The museum borrowed an old, very famous and very expensive necklace with diamonds and rubies for the exhibit called the Van Camp necklace. It's magnificent, and everyone was looking at it last night."

"Well that's simple. It was probably misplaced," says Alex. "Maybe when someone put it down, it fell on the floor, got kicked under a chair or something, and Mr. Howard just hasn't looked there yet."

Dad smiles at the twins. "That's possible, except that the necklace was in a special case with a big glass cover over it, and an alarm. Nobody could touch it."

"Well, Hank, that's not exactly correct." Mom has something on her mind.

"What do you mean?" Dad looks at Mom with a puzzled expression.

"Don't you remember when the photographer for the newspaper wanted to get a picture of Beatrice wearing the family necklace?"

"You're right. John had to get the security guard from the front to turn off the alarm, but I'm sure it was returned to the case before John closed up."

I'm not sure I understand what's going on.

"Who's Beatrice?" the twins demand.

"She's the current Mrs. Van Camp. The necklace was created over a hundred years ago for Mr. Van Camp's grandmother."

"Cool."

"Not so cool if it's missing," Dad says. "I promised John I would go over to the museum and help him figure out what happened."

"Can we go?" both Veronica and Alex ask together.

Me, too! Me, too! If I get my leash, maybe he'll get the hint.

"Okay. And we'll take Upton. It'll be a nice walk."

Yippee!

"Walk? Can't we drive?" says Veronica. "Get dressed, couch potatoes," Dad says, smiling. "We're leaving in thirty minutes, and your rooms have to be picked up."

"I'm sure there is some logical explanation, Hank," Mom says. She doesn't sound convincing.

CHAPTER THREE
Off to the Museum

We're going on an outing, and I have never been to a museum before. Come to think about it, I'm not exactly sure what happens at a museum. I do know there are different kinds of museums and that we're going to an art museum in which, I assume, there are paintings and things. Anyway, I am excited.

"Veronica, Alex, come on, we've got to go," Dad shouts up the stairs. Sometimes he forgets the twins listen to the radio in their rooms and can't hear him. Then he gets angry and shouts again. Mom will say something like, "Hank, you should go upstairs and turn the music volume down before you yell," but he usually shouts again anyway.

Dad looks at his watch. The twins may not be ready, but I won't be late. I amble over to the chair where they put my leash and patiently sit.

A loud noise fills the house. No big deal, it's only the twins thundering down the stairs. They sound like elephants, or at least what I imagine elephants must sound like running down stairs. I have never personally heard an elephant. Dad sometimes says that the kids sound like them when they are wearing their shoes in the house. While no one is looking, I jump on the chair, grab my leash, and calmly walk over to Dad.

"Good boy, Upton. I see you're ready to go. Come on, gang. I've promised Mr. Howard that I would meet him in fifteen minutes and we are NOT going to take the car. Coats on, it's still chilly outside."

"We're coming," they reply.

Dad clips the leash onto my collar and I am ready for a walk. I don't know how long we'll be gone, because I don't know how far it is to the museum.

"How long do you think you'll be?" Mom asks.

"About an hour. Maybe a little more. I'll stop on the way back and get the kids a hot chocolate," Dad says.

"Can I get a milkshake instead?" Alex asks.

13

The twins must have the best ears in the world, because they aren't even in the same room as Mom and Dad.

"We'll discuss it later. Just get your coats on," Dad announces.

"I think I'll slip out and do some errands. Okay?" Mom asks.

"Great idea. I'll do things with the kids until noon, and then we'll be back for lunch."

"Can we get pizza?" Veronica yells from the front hall.

"There is certainly nothing wrong with their hearing," Mom says, laughing.

Dad grabs the leash.

"We're out of here." He gives Mom a kiss.

There is still a little bit of snow on the ground, but the air is warm. I love spring. A walk to the museum is a great idea. We meet several very nice people and a couple of dogs, who are all bigger than I am, but then again most dogs are bigger than me. But I don't worry too much about that—it's really hard to get mad at a twelve-pound, white, fluffy dog, especially one who wags his tail a lot.

We walk past the bank, the camera store, and some stores that sell clothes. I can't read yet, so unless Dad or the twins tell me the name of the store, I'm out of luck, since they all look the same to me, except, of course, stores that sell food. I am especially fond of bakeries, although dogs are not supposed to go into food stores and I can't understand why. Sometimes Mom will pick me up and carry me into some fabulous place, especially if she is in a hurry. People are usually very nice to me, and I am nice to them. I don't bark. Sometimes I sneeze if I know they've got treats for me, but I never bark. I am entirely too polite.

Our walk to the museum is brisk. Although I explore and smell everything, Dad keeps us moving along. Occasionally I do something else along the way, like every other dog.

We cross a busy intersection after the light changes and walk down a very pretty street lined with big old trees and even bigger buildings.

"How much farther?" Veronica starts to whine.

Who cares? It's a beautiful day for a walk. Alex grabs some snow.

"Alex, don't even think about it. Veronica, please stop complaining. It's a gorgeous day for a walk," Dad tells her.

Alex looks at his snowball and then at his sister.

"Dad, Alex is going to throw a snowball at me," Veronica says and gives her brother a little punch, though not very hard.

"Was not," Alex replies.

"Stop it!" Dad says. "Or I will leave you outside and take Upton in with me."

"No!" the twins shriek. "We want to help find the Van Camp necklace."

"Okay, but no fighting."

They nod in agreement.

We turn into the driveway of a two-story brick building with a porch that goes around the front. I guess this is the museum. The first thing I see is a police car. It doesn't look like Mr. Howard from the museum has discovered the necklace yet. We're still in time to help.

"Looks as if it's going to be a busy day," Dad says.

CHAPTER FOUR
Searching for Clues

Several grown-ups are busy talking to one another in front of the museum: a policeman in his blue uniform, an older gentleman with a bushy white beard wearing a blazer and a big bow tie, and a younger man with very short hair wearing a tee shirt with a picture of a bird on it.

"Hank, it's very good to see you. Thanks for coming. Brought the whole gang with you, I see." It is the man with the white beard. He shakes hands with Dad.

"Kids, I'd like you to meet the director of the museum, Mr. John Howard," Dad says. The twins extend their hands which Mr. Howard shakes. I sit and raise my paw. "And this is Upton."

Mr. Howard leans over and shakes my paw. He is smiling too.

"So, John, what's going on?" Dad asks.

"Let's all go inside and I'll show you," Mr. Howard replies.

We start to walk into the building, except the policeman who goes back to his car. The museum director abruptly stops. "Hank, the dog shouldn't really go in."

"I promise you he won't bark, and after all the trees he visited on the way over here he won't have an accident. Anyway, I'm not going to leave him outside. If you're insistent, I'll take him back home with the children and come back later."

Yay, Dad. You're my hero.

"No!" Mr. Howard says quickly. "I really need you here, now. I guess the dog won't be a problem. He's a little dog anyway."

Hey, I'm three years old and I weigh twelve pounds but if being little gets me into the museum it's perfectly fine with me. The twins have been very quiet, and they are never quiet. I hope they are feeling all right.

"Dad?" Veronica whispers. "Can we see a picture of the Van Camp necklace so that we know what we're looking for?"

An excellent suggestion.

"John, do you have a photograph of the necklace?" Dad asks Mr. Howard.

18

The young man, who is standing next to Mr. Howard answers by nodding his head. I wonder what his name is.

"Good idea, Hank." Mr. Howard turns to the young man. "Chris, do you remember the name of the photographer who took pictures of Mrs. Van Camp wearing the necklace last night?"

"Yes, I'll give her a call and ask her to make several copies," Chris replies. "I'll make arrangements for the pictures to be delivered as soon as possible."

The man named Chris leaves and goes into another part of the museum.

"Follow me," Mr. Howard says.

We enter a very large room filled with paintings hanging on the walls. Each painting is mounted in a gold frame...I wonder why? The twins are impressed. They walk toward a painting of two girls wearing large straw hats, sitting next to each other drawing pictures. Veronica and Alex stop and stare at the colorful image.

"The artist's name is Pierre-Auguste Renoir," Mr. Howard says, coming up behind the girls. He pronounces the name like this: Pea-air Aww-gust Ren-waa. "He lived in France in the late 1800s and early 1900s. He is a very famous artist, and is considered to be one of the founders of a style of painting called Impressionism."

"It's really beautiful. When I move, the painting seems to change color." Veronica says with excitement.

"It's interesting, Hank," Mr. Howard continues. "Your children were immediately

19

attracted to one of the most famous paintings in our entire collection."

Dad nods in agreement and begins to amble toward them.

"Children," Mr. Howard calls out. "Can you guess what Renoir named this painting?"

The twins look at each other, then at the painting, and then at Mr. Howard. They shrug their shoulders.

"Twins," he tells them.

They smile.

"This room features the works of many Impressionists: Edouard Manet, Claude Monet, and Edgar Degas. It's my favorite room."

"It's mine, too!" Alex exclaims.

I never knew Alex had been to a museum before.

"We really need to go, but both of you may come back any time," Mr. Howard offers. "I will personally give you a tour".

"Can we, can we, Dad?" the twins reply together.

"Of course, and a private tour with one of the nation's most famous art historians would be pretty special, I'd say." Dad winks.

There is definitely a disadvantage to being a dog. We are color blind—which means we can't see things in different colors. That doesn't mean I don't appreciate all these paintings...they are awesome even in black and white.

Mr. Howard leads us into another room, which is filled with paintings, but mostly photographs. There are also dresses, coats and hats displayed on plastic things that sort of look like people you see in the clothing store windows. Books and dishes and lots of other things are set out on tables around the room, which I cannot see because they are too high.

In the middle of the room is a tall box with a glass top, which Mom said held the necklace. There are two men in police uniforms standing near the box. I want to look inside to see if there are any clues. Maybe I can check out the necklace, but then I remember it is gone, which is why we are at the museum...to find the Van Camp necklace.

"As soon as the officers are done dusting for fingerprints we can look more closely," Mr. Howard tells Dad.

"Have you called the chief?" Dad looks at John.

"Yes, I called Chief O'Brien and his brother Jerry."

"Why Jerry?"

Dad has a funny look on his face.

"We bought a special insurance policy for the show. Otherwise the Van Camps would not have loaned us the necklace for display. Jerry is the insurance agent."

"Were you able to reach either of them?" Dad says rapidly.

"Not yet."

"John, one simple question: What does the museum stand to lose if the necklace has indeed been stolen?"

Dad's question confuses me. How could the museum lose anything if someone else's necklace

21

is stolen?

"I don't think we're going to suffer any real loss, except that in the future people won't trust us with their expensive things to put on exhibit."

The twins and I are standing in the back of the room, and none of this makes any sense to us... or at least to me. Let's just look for the necklace. Chris enters the room and walks over to John.

"Mr. Howard," he says. "Excuse me, but Chief O'Brien just called and said that he's on his way over to the museum and he is with his brother. They expect to be here in about fifteen minutes."

"We're done," says one of the policemen. "We found lots of fingerprints, but I'm not sure how helpful they will be, because it looks as though everyone touched the case during last evening's event. If you have any questions, the chief will be able to tell you everything. We'll call him and let him know what we've found."

"Thanks," replies Mr. Howard to the police officers.

Are fingerprints like paw prints?

Mr. Howard and Dad walk over to the case. Alex and Veronica look at each other.

"Let's go explore," Veronica suggests.

We all agree. The case in which the necklace had been on display is tall. Well, everything seems tall to me, but it is almost as tall as the twins. And then there is a glass case on top. I want to see the top of the case, but no one offers to pick me up. Okay, I'll look around on the floor.

"There are no signs of anyone entering the

museum after I locked up last night," Mr. Howard tells Dad. "The alarm was still activated when I opened up this morning. There are no broken windows or open doors. The necklace is simply missing."

Mr. Howard's voice is very soft. Dad looks around the room, then up. The girls and I follow Dad's eyes. The ceiling has a skylight.

"Dad, do you think someone could have opened the skylight during the night and climbed down, opened the case, stolen the necklace and climbed back up?" Veronica asks, following an imaginary line from the case to the skylight.

"Maybe the thief used a rope ladder. I saw that once in a movie," Alex adds.

"Excellent thoughts, children," Mr. Howard says.

Well, actually he says to the twins, although it was my idea also. Maybe we all saw the same movie.

"The problem is the skylight is connected to the alarm system," Mr. Howard says. "Also, I sent Chris up to the roof early this morning, and he said that no one had been up there. The police went up later and made the same observation."
I wonder how they could tell.

"How did they know that no one had been up there?" Dad seems to be thinking the same thing as me.

"Because there's still some snow on the roof and there are no footprints."

Good answer. This is fun. It's like a game where we eliminate people and places, like Clue.

"Dad, I've got a good idea." Alex pulls on Dad's sleeve.

He looks at him. "Yes?"

"If no one came into the museum last night after everyone left, then the necklace must have been taken during the party."

"That seems logical, but who took the necklace and why? And when Mr. Howard locked up last night, the necklace was in the case when he left."

"Well...not exactly," Mr. Howard says, shaking his head. "I didn't actually look at the necklace before I left last night. In fact, I didn't look at it after I put it away after the photographs were shot."

"That doesn't really affect the question of who took the necklace and why," Dad says.

"But didn't you say it was very expensive?" Veronica asks. "That must have been the reason for stealing it."

"Yes," Dad nods. "But it is also very famous and would be hard to sell once word got out it was stolen. You couldn't even wear it out in public."

This is frustrating. Why steal something if you can't sell it or wear it?

"I would hate to think that anyone who came to the museum for a benefit event would steal something on exhibit," Dad says.

If people steal things from a museum, other people won't get the chance to see them.

"Remember, Hank," Mr. Howard replies, "the jewelry is insured."

"John, other than you and the Van Camps,

who knew that?" Dad wants to know.

"Jerry O'Brien," Mr. Howard says. "His company insured the necklace."

Chris returns and says, "Chief O'Brien and Mr. O'Brien are here."

"Thank you. Please ask them to join us."

CHAPTER FIVE
Upton Makes a Discovery

Two very large men stomp into the room. Their voices are as large as they are. They look a lot alike. They are not identical twins, but they are obviously brothers.

One of the men is dressed in a fancy-looking policeman's uniform with gold trim on his shiny black cap and down his arms and legs. He must be the chief. His face is large, with red cheeks and bushy eyebrows that waggle up and down. His belly sticks out like he is hiding a basketball under his uniform.

The other man, also large and round, is wearing a leather jacket and jeans. He looks very worried.

"Chief, Jerry...glad you could get here so fast," Mr. Howard exclaims.

"I got your message," says the man wearing the uniform. "Jerry and I were together, so we thought we would come by and take a look. Any ideas?"

The chief glances at the twins and then at me.

"Brought out all the troops, eh, Hank? Do you think we'll need a bloodhound to find this necklace?"

The chief starts to laugh at his dumb joke. I am not a bloodhound. I don't appreciate that he is making fun of the twins either. I can sense that Dad is about to say something, but he decides not to. Probably a good idea.

"Other than what I assume your officers told you, there is not a lot I can add," Mr. Howard says. "Everything was locked up last night, and when I got here this morning the Van Camp necklace was gone. There are no signs that anyone broke into the museum last night. The necklace has simply vanished."

Both Chief O'Brien and his brother walk up close to the case and lift the glass. I hear a high-pitched sound. It hurts my ears. Dogs are more sensitive to that kind of sound than humans, but I can tell that everyone else also hears the noise because Dad asks, "What's that?"

"The case is attached to an alarm system," Mr. Howard tells us. "There are three positions for the alarm: off, silent, which you just heard, and full alarm, that makes a very loud noise and automatically calls both the alarm company and the police. That's the problem. The alarm system never went off last night, not even the silent alarm, but the necklace is nevertheless gone."

"When Mrs. Van Camp was wearing the necklace I didn't hear the sound," Dad says to everyone.

"When we took out the necklace for her to wear for the photographs, I turned off the alarm," Mr. Howard tells us. "But to anticipate your question, I'm sure I turned it back on, first to silent for the rest of the party, and then set it to full alarm, along with the alarms for the rest of the museum when we left."

"We?" asks Dad.

"Yes, I left with the Van Camps," Mr. Howard says. "We were the last ones to leave. I thought it was very nice of them to stay so late. We chatted quite a while."

At last, Jerry starts to speak. "I'll need you to fill out a report for the insurance company on Monday. They're going to be upset because the company really didn't want to insure the necklace in the first place."

"How much is the necklace worth?" Veronica asks.

"Well, young lady, it is extremely difficult to place a value on something like the Van Camp necklace. Since it was going to be on exhibit in a museum and not worn in public, the insurance company estimated its value at about two million dollars."

"Wow, that's a ton of money!" Alex looks excited at the thought.

"Who is the beneficiary of the policy?" Dad questions.

I am not sure exactly what Dad means by that, but Mr. Howard quickly tells us, "The Van Camps will receive the insurance money."

"Something doesn't add up," the chief says. "Since the Van Camp necklace is such a well-known and unique piece of jewelry, I presume it will be extremely difficult for a thief to sell."

Dad walks over to the case. "Not if the necklace is broken up for its stones. If each diamond and ruby is taken out of the necklace, a thief could actually make quite a lot of money. Jerry, any idea how much the necklace would be worth as individual diamonds and rubies?"

"I have no idea, but I'm sure we can find out," Jerry says, scratching his head. "I don't know how the insurance company valued the piece for determining the amount of coverage. Sometimes the value is based on how much it would cost to replace the necklace if it is lost or stolen, rather than how much you could sell the necklace for to someone else. I just don't know."

This is all a little confusing to me, but I do understand that the Van Camp necklace is worth a lot of money, and it's gone. Let's stop talking and begin looking. I decide to walk around the room and check it out. I start to leave the group of talking grown-ups, but Alex is still holding my leash. I give a tug. He looks down, and then looks back up to listen. I pull again. I know that he doesn't want to be bothered, so he does exactly what I thought he would do. He drops the end of the leash on the floor, and I am now free to walk around and examine the room. I may not be a bloodhound, but remember, I have a terrific sense of smell. The only thing that I don't know is, what does a necklace smell like? Even if it's just metal and stones, it will still have a smell...to a dog.

I start to walk away from the display case when the chief says, "There goes your bloodhound, hot on the trail." He laughs again, but I still don't think he's funny.

"Hey guys, will one of you make sure to hold on to Upton's leash? I don't want him to get into anything he is not supposed to."

That's just the point, Dad, I need to explore. Wait, what's this? Veronica approaches and picks up my leash. No! Look what I've found. I am not going to go anywhere. Veronica is in a hurry to get back to the group surrounding the case, but I am not going to move until somebody looks at what I have found.

"Upton, come on!"

I am not going to move until she looks at what I have found. Veronica starts to drag me across the floor. It doesn't hurt because the floor is slippery, but I am getting angry. Just stop and look. It's important. Come on, Veronica, I look at your things. Just stop. This is turning into a tug of war.

"Veronica," Alex shouts, "you're hurting Upton."

Well, that got everyone's attention. Yip!

"What's wrong?" Dad walks over.

Veronica, who hasn't done anything wrong is being blamed for doing exactly what Dad has asked her to do, throws down the leash. "You take him. He won't come with me."

Uh oh, Dad seems upset. I quickly scamper back to my discovery and sit. Everyone is looking at me now, and I get the feeling that I am about to be removed from the museum. Wait! Look!

As Dad bends over to pick up the end of the leash, I lie down. Usually, whenever anyone picks up my leash I get excited. Dad stares at me. Then finally, at long last, he looks down at my discovery.

"What's this, Upton?" He picks up what I have found. He turns it around in his fingers and then holds it up to the light. Mr. Howard and the Chief are now next to Dad. "Gentlemen and lady, Upton has provided us with an interesting piece to the puzzle."

"What is it, Hank?" Mr. Howard nearly steps on me to see what Dad is holding.

"A diamond!" Dad holds up the gemstone between his fingers so that everyone can see. "The question is, where did it come from?"

"May I look at that?" Jerry joins us.

Dad hands him the diamond. Mr. O'Brien carefully looks at the stone. He turns it over and over. "It's not right. It doesn't shine like a diamond. I'll bet it's a fake." O'Brien hands the gem back to Dad.

31

"You mean like costume jewelry?" Alex asks.

"Yes, but better. It is a real good copy and well-cut, but I bet it's not a real diamond."

"Hey, everybody, who cares?" the chief asks. "It probably fell off of someone's fake jewelry last night. You know, a lot of rich people keep the original stuff in the bank and wear fake so that they won't get robbed."

The chief is probably right, but it was worth finding. I'll look for something else. Since no one has picked up my leash, I'll just sneak away and explore the display case while everyone else is looking at the diamond...or whatever it is. Let's see, basic wooden case, nothing interesting, except it smells like Mom when she goes out with Dad, but not quite the same. I walk around and around. Something is not quite right. It's almost at the bottom of the case. Hey Dad, come over here!

No surprise, he doesn't hear me. Yip! I yip again and again. Now I've got his attention. I almost never bark, so he knows I've found something else.

Dad quickly comes over to the case. I think that maybe everyone is listening to me now in a human kind of way. Hey, Dad, check out the bottom of the case. He just looks at me. Well, I've got to be more obvious. I start to scratch the case along the bottom edge, on the side that smells. Dad gets down on his knees and looks. He moves his hand up and down the side of the case. He stops. He pushes and then pulls. A drawer opens up. Oh, my gosh, guess what's inside the drawer?

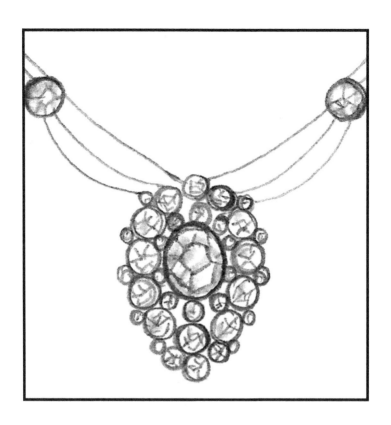

CHAPTER SIX
The Necklace is Found

It really is spectacular. Dad stares. Everyone rushes over and moves so near that the case nearly falls over. Carefully, Dad removes the drawer. He just looks at the Van Camp necklace. He cannot believe it. Yeah, I knew it. The grownups forgot where they had put it.

"Dad, can we see?" scream the twins, who are standing on their tiptoes to look over Dad's shoulder.

The chief and his brother begin to push

them aside, which I think is a very rude thing to do. The necklace isn't going anywhere, at least for a few minutes.

"Wow!" For all that shoving, the chief doesn't have much to say.

"Hank, may I please see the necklace?" Mr. Howard wants his turn, too.

Dad presents the drawer to Mr. Howard, who is now sitting in a chair near the door. He looks very tired.

Mr. Howard smiles when Dad gives him the necklace. "I am greatly relieved. I was quite worried that all the good work we've tried to do at the museum would be wasted if someone had actually stolen the Van Camp necklace, especially with all the security we've installed."

The twins walk over to Dad. "May we see?"

"Hank, let them have a look. If it weren't for their dog, I don't know how long it would have been before we recovered the necklace." Mr. Howard smiles.

How long? Without me, they never would have found the necklace. They never would have even looked for it in the right place. Hey, I want to see it again, too.

"Can we touch it?" Veronica asks.

"Chief," Dad calls out. "Can we take the necklace from the drawer?"

"I'm sure it's okay. There won't be any fingerprints on an item like that anyway, and the outside of the drawer was dusted when my men were here, only they didn't see the secret door. Hank, maybe you could rent me your hound whenever anything is missing?" The chief chuckles.

No way, José. I only help out family...and friends. No police work for me. I've got certain standards. I am strictly private.

Dad carefully removes the necklace from the drawer and shows it to the twins.

"Can I try it on?" Veronica pleads.

Alex shakes his head.

Dad makes a funny face. He raises one of his eyebrows as if to say, "You've got to be kidding."

I gaze at the necklace. It is exquisite, but it would not look good as a dog collar, so I'm not interested in trying it on. Hey, Dad, better look at the necklace again...very carefully.

I sneeze. It works. Dad holds up the famous Van Camp necklace. I see it, or rather, I don't see it. Look Dad...look! Not being able to talk to humans sometimes has its drawbacks. I watch Dad move his fingers over the necklace. He stops. Yes!

"Jerry!" Dad says. "Do you know a good jeweler? One who knows fine gems, and one you could reach now?"

Everyone stares at Dad.

"I imagine Walter Jacobi will be in his store this morning," Jerry says. "Why?"

"Please call Mr. Jacobi and ask him if he'd come over here as soon as he's available. Tell him it is of the utmost importance, and ask him not to discuss this with anyone. We need him to look at a piece of jewelry to see if it is genuine or not."

Everyone is quiet. I am very glad Dad finally examined the necklace.

"Hank, what are you talking about?"

Mr. Howard stands.

"Who has the stone that Upton found on the floor?" Dad glances at each of the assembled group.

"Why, I do," Jerry O'Brien says, pulling the diamond I found out of his pocket.

"You said you think that this may not be real?" Dad isn't really getting to the point very quickly.

Dad puts the necklace back into the drawer and walks over to Jerry O'Brien, who hands him the stone, which Dad in turn fits into a missing section of the necklace.

"Charlie, you had better take a look at this," Mr. O'Brien says to his brother, the chief.

Panicked, Mr. Howard declares, "What is it?"

"The stone that Upton found, which Jerry believes may not be real, fits perfectly into an empty place on the necklace."

"Meaning the Van Camp necklace is a fake?" Mr. Howard's face turns red and I begin to worry about his health. He should go back to the chair and sit down.

"For right now it means nothing," Dad says. "Certainly we need to collect some additional facts about the necklace. First, we don't know whether what I'm holding is genuine or not, or if the stone that fell out is simply a replacement for one lost years ago and not a portion of the original piece."

"I'd better go make the call to Mr. Jacobi." Mr. O'Brien is nearly out of breath, although he hasn't even moved. He takes out a cell phone from his pocket and moves to a corner of the room.

Dad looks down at me and winks.

The man called Chris rushes into the room again, holding several pieces of paper. "The pho- tographer e-mailed me copies of the digital pictures she took last night, and I printed them on the color printer. They actually came out pretty well. I was lucky to get the pictures so quickly. I've got copies for everyone."

Chris busily hands them out. He doesn't give me one. What does he think I am doing around here, anyway? At least I have convinced Dad to listen to me.

"Well, we know one thing for sure." Chief O'Brien waits until he is sure everyone is paying attention.

He is a very self-centered person. Okay, Chief, everyone is finally looking at you.

"The necklace you are holding, Hank, is the same necklace that Mrs. Van Camp had on last night!" Chief O'Brien pauses and then adds, "when the photos were taken, the fake diamond, or whatever it is, had previously fallen out of the setting."

"Chief," Dad cautions, "we don't want to jump to conclusions. Although it's logical that the stone fell out when Mrs. Van Camp was being photographed, we still don't know why it was hidden in the drawer. Nor do we know if the entire necklace, or for that matter, even the stone we... Upton...found, is real or fake. I think Mr. Jacobi will provide the answer to several key questions which will probably only force us to ask many more questions."

Mr. O'Brien rushes over. "He'll be here in about ten minutes."

Great! Then we'll get some answers.

"Can I try on the necklace now?"

Veronica never gives up.

"Why not?" Mr. Howard agrees. Veronica claps her hands, while Alex walks away.

I guess this is like playing in Mom's dressing room, but even better. This is the Van Camp necklace, after all.

Or is it?

CHAPTER SEVEN
The Necklace--Real or Fake?

Veronica looks really terrific wearing the Van Camp necklace, or whatever it is. She struts around like royalty, while Alex is clearly disgusted with his sister's showing-off. Everyone is eagerly waiting for Mr. Jacobi to arrive.

I wonder if I should look for other clues. I think I'll hold off until we know a little more about the necklace. What can I do while we wait? Maybe I can get Dad's attention and see if he'll take off my leash which I am dragging around. Let's see, bark, whine, sneeze, or...I got it. I walk over to Dad and begin to push his leg. He is talking to Mr. Howard. Hello, Dad.

"Yes, Upton," he says as he finally looks down at me. "Your leash. I don't think you need it."

"So far, your little pooch has made all our discoveries by just roaming around. Maybe we should put him on the payroll."

Mr. Howard appears to feel a lot better than he did a few minutes ago.

Thanks for the compliment, but remember, I am strictly private.

"Walter! Thank you for coming over at such short notice," Jerry O'Brien says as someone new walks into the museum. He walks over to shake Walter's hand. "I would like you all to meet Walter Jacobi, who, I hope will answer our most pressing question...is the necklace real or fake?"

Mr. Jacobi is a short, dark-haired man with slick black hair, a tiny little mustache and bright blue eyes. He is wearing a dark grey suit with a pretty necktie with flowers all over.

Dad walks over to greet Mr. Jacobi, who looks very young for someone who is going to tell us about the Van Camp necklace. Veronica quickly puts the necklace back into the drawer and joins us. Alex gives her a little shove.

"Walter, do you know my little brother Charlie?"

Little? Now that's a laugh.

"Chief." Mr. Jacobi shakes his hand.

"And of course you know John Howard, the

40

museum's director, Hank Charles, and his brood."

Dad continues with the introductions. "I'd like you to meet my children, Veronica and Alex... and our dog Upton, without whose keen eye...and nose we might never have found whatever it is you're about to see. Kids, where is the necklace, anyway?"

"She's got it," Alex announces as Veronica hands the drawer to Mr. Jacobi.

Dad puts the small stone that I found back into the drawer.

"Do you have a desk or table with good light?" Mr. Jacobi asks.

"You can use my office," Mr. Howard offers. "I'll show you the way."

As Mr. Jacobi and Mr. Howard turn to leave, Mr. Jacobi says to the twins, "Do you kids want to come with us? I'll show you how to tell whether the necklace is genuine or not."

"Cool. Thanks," the twins reply.

I think I'll go, too.

Looking down at Alex and Veronica, Mr. Jacobi says, "I know your mother. She's been coming into our store for a long time, even before you were born."

Hurry up! Let's go! Real or fake?

Mr. Howard leads us toward his office, which he announces is on the second floor of the museum. It may not sound like a big deal to you, but climbing up all those slippery marble steps is far more difficult than you think, especially for a little dog. No one offers to pick me up and carry me, I might add. Well, I wanted to come along—no

41

pain, no gain.

We turn left at the top of the stairs and walk the entire length of the building until we finally arrive at Mr. Howard's office, which is not what I expected. I imagined a room with high ceilings, wood paneling, and heavy, dark, antique furniture. Probably a lot of art books scattered on various tables. In any event, I am totally wrong. I wonder where I get my ideas sometimes, since I've never even been in a museum director's office before. I haven't even been in a museum until today. Too much television, no doubt. Mr. Howard's office is entirely white, except for a light beige carpet. It is filled with computer equipment and filing cabinets.

"Wow, this place looks like Houston space center," Veronica says. "Look at all the awesome stuff."

"That's the biggest monitor I have ever seen," Alex adds.

"Very impressive, very impressive," Mr. Jacobi nods.

"Thank you. I'm slightly embarrassed. I got the computer bug about fifteen years ago, and I'm now almost out of control. I read all the magazines, the ones for people who use computers and the ones for people who design computers. I always want the latest and the fastest and the biggest."

He smiles at the twins. "I found that once we brought the museum into the technology age, we are able to better manage our collections. If another museum wants to display an exhibit, we know in an instant whether we have anything we can loan them. We've catalogued everything. We're able to rotate exhibits so people are able to see all the wonderful pieces that have been given to the museum over the years. I can tell you how long any painting has been hanging on a wall and how many people have come into the museum during that period of time. Anyway, I think all this equipment is way fun to play with."

The kids look thrilled. Mr. Howard has just made two new friends.

"Do you play a lot of games?" Alex asks.

"Sometimes, but only after I've finished all my work. Do you children want to come over some day after school and mess with the computer?" The twins examine a long bench absolutely filled with every possible gadget any high tech geek could imagine. "We'd love to!"

"Mr. Howard, do you have a place where I can take a close look at the necklace?" Mr. Jacobi asks. "I'll need a good light and a clear surface."

Mr. Jacobi is eager to get to work. I can't blame him.

"Yes, of course. Sorry. I love to talk computers, but we really must do first things first, and first we need to check out the Van Camp necklace."

Mr. Howard picks up what looks like a TV remote control and pushes a button. Like magic, the room is flooded in light. He walks over to the wall across from the computers and reaches up and pulls down a part of the wall, folding it into a table. No kidding. It's a hidden table. One second it is the wall, and the next second it becomes a table. Mr. Howard brings over a small lamp and a wooden chair, turns to Mr. Jacobi and inquires, "Will this do?"

"Perfect. Okay everyone, gather around. I want you to understand what it is I'm going to do." Mr. Jacobi places the necklace on the table, together with the loose stone. He reaches into his coat pocket and pulls out a black case, which he opens. He removes a pair of tweezers and picks up the little stone, and places it into the necklace.

"Obviously, we have a perfect fit. That's the first question we needed to answer. Veronica, what's another question you think we ought to answer?"

"Well, is the necklace real or pretend?"

"All of it or part?" Mr. Jacobi says, trying to make this into a guessing game.

"What do you mean?" Veronica asks.

"I know, I know," Alex shouts. "The next thing we need to find out is if the diamond Upton found is real."

"Very good."

Alex looks very pleased with himself.

"However," Mr. Jacobi adds, "I don't think we should call it a diamond until we can prove it's a diamond. Until then, we will call it *the stone*. Okay?"

The twins nod and...well, I wag my tail. This is a terrific way to spend a morning. Mr. Jacobi takes a round thing out of his case and puts it on his eye.

"This is called a jeweler's loupe. It is a magnifying lens that helps me look at the stone more closely. A diamond has several unique qualities

44

that make it different from, say, glass. Jewelers talk about diamonds in terms of their quality or perfection, color, cut, and size. But we can't talk about the stone in those terms until we prove that it is a diamond."

"Well, how can you do that?" Alex asks.

"A diamond is a piece of carbon that has been put under extreme pressure and heat over millions of years. Two important things: a diamond is one of the hardest things on earth. That means a diamond can scratch something without being damaged. Secondly, when light passes through a diamond, it bends the light, and you can see a pattern."

"Like a rainbow?" Veronica says.

"Yes, exactly. Wow, you kids are really smart. I am impressed."

So am I.

"Are all diamonds made into jewelry?" Alex wonders.

"As a matter of fact, only a small portion of all the diamonds mined are used for jewelry, about twenty percent," Mr. Jacobi answers.

"What happens to the rest?" Veronica asks.

"Because diamonds are so hard, they have many industrial uses, mostly as cutting or polishing tools."

"When I was a young man," Mr. Howard adds, "diamonds were used as needles for phonographic records. But now you have CDs and DVDs, and they use lasers."

"Starting around 1970, companies began to manufacture synthetic, or man-made, diamonds, and that's what we're looking for."   Mr. Jacobi removes his glasses.

Mr. Jacobi holds the stone under the light and studies it for a few minutes. He moves the light over toward the necklace. Finally, he puts it down.

Real or fake?

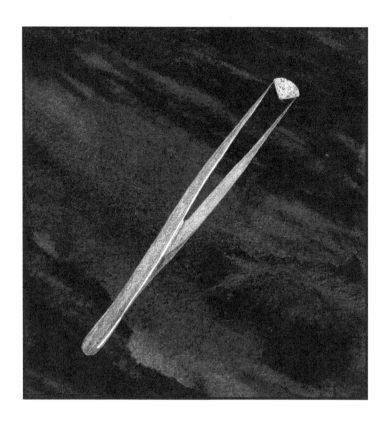

CHAPTER EIGHT
More Questions and Few Answers

"The stone is not a diamond. It is an excellent imitation, but it is not genuine," Mr. Jacobi announces.

We all look at Mr. Howard. He is doing the same thing Dad does...he raises one eyebrow. I wish dogs could do that.

"Mr. Jacobi—" Mr. Howard starts to pace back and forth.

"Please call me Walter. Whenever someone calls me Mr. Jacobi, I think they're looking for my father."

"Fine. Please call me John. Now, Walter, what about the rest of the necklace?"

"It appears to be an imitation as well. While I am not 100 per cent certain without further testing, I am 99 per cent certain. The setting is also not authentic. It is very high quality, but is certainly not original. I suspect that the entire necklace was made abroad, probably the Far East, within the last ten years, maybe the last five years. Also, I suspect that it was made by copying the original, not merely a photograph, but the actual Van Camp necklace. Someone took a lot of time and went to a lot of expense to create this replica."

"I think we had better share your findings with the group downstairs."

Again, Mr. Howard doesn't sound so good.

We retrace our steps down the long hall toward the slippery staircase. It looks even scarier going down. One missed step and I am going to crash and hurt myself. I stop for a second and try to figure this out.

"Here, Upton, I'll carry you down so you won't fall."

Thank you, Alex...thank you.

Dad and the O'Briens greet us, as we walk in. They are all drinking coffee and eating donuts. Maybe I should have stayed down here and gotten a handout. No. I am glad I went upstairs.

"What's your verdict?" Jerry O'Brien asks Walter.

"Fake, but a good fake, a very good fake," says Mr. Jacobi. "The necklace was made sometime in the last ten years. Jerry, did the insurance company have someone examine the necklace before they issued the insurance?"

"A good question," the chief mumbles between bites of his donut.

"Actually, no, they didn't." Jerry O'Brien states.

"Actually, yes, they did," Mr. Howard chimes in. "After we set up the exhibit on Wednesday, two men from the insurance company came to the museum. One was a security expert who wanted to see our entire system, and the other introduced himself as an appraiser. He closely inspected the necklace."

"Wow, that is weird," Mr. O'Brien says. "Usually the insurance company tells me in advance when any of their people are going to visit someone to whom I've sold insurance."

Dad finally says something. "John, how do you know they were actually from the insurance company?"

I think I see where Dad is heading.

"Oh, they said they were, and furthermore, one of them gave me his card. They called to schedule our meeting several days in advance. It made sense to me."

"Hank, where are you going with this?" the chief questions.

"John," Dad begins, "do you still have the insurance man's business card?"

"Of course," Mr. Howard replies. "I made a copy and placed it in a file with all the other insurance papers concerning the Van Camp exhibit.

I put the card in a notebook I keep with all of the calling cards I've been given over the years, just in case I want to find the person again. Do you want to see the original card or the copy?"

"If it is not too much of a problem, I would like to see the original," Dad says. "Jerry, have you ever seen a calling card from the insurance company?"

Dad really seems like he's onto something now.

"I'm positive I have. People from the main

office are always coming in to see me, usually to ask me to sell something." Mr. O'Brien looks at Dad with a very confused expression on his face.

The chief jumps into the discussion. "Hank, what are you driving at here?"

"Gentlemen and lady, it seems to me that for the same reason we needed to find out if the necklace is genuine or not, I think we had better find out whether the men who said they were from the insurance company are genuine or not."

Dad is on a roll now.

Mr. Howard almost faints. "Hank, are you saying the men I let examine the necklace and our security system might have been involved in the disappearance of the necklace?"

"I'm sorry, John, but that is exactly what may have happened."

Mr. Howard shakes his fists in the air and grumbles, "I'll never forgive myself."

"John, please get me the card, and Jerry, could you get a sample card from the insurance company?"

"Now?" Mr. O'Brien asks.

"Yes, if it isn't too much of a problem. I want to compare the cards. This will at least give us some idea of whether these men are really representatives from the insurance company, or part of the problem."

"It'll only take a few minutes." Mr. O'Brien briskly walks away.

"I'll get my calling card book from my office," Mr. Howard tells Dad.

"Walter, how long will it take you to be com- pletely certain regarding the authenticity of the necklace?" Dad asks the jeweler.

"No more than an hour. I want to look closely at each stone. However, I'd prefer to take the necklace back to my store. At the same time, I'll do a little research to see if I can figure out where this copy came from and when it was made."

"That's great. Chief...since this is a very important piece of evidence, don't you think an officer should go with Walter, so that no one can say that the real necklace was stolen while in Mr. Jacobi's possession?"

Dad is being very cautious.

"An excellent idea, Hank. I'll get a patrol-man here in a couple of minutes."

With Mr. Howard and Mr. O'Brien, and now the chief and Mr. Jacobi, out of the room, everything seems so quiet. Maybe I'll take a look around. Never know what I will find.

CHAPTER NINE
An Alarming Development

I think a dog's-eye examination of the entire room should be conducted. I have learned from Dad that it is best to be methodical, so I must do everything in order. I'll start at the door and walk around the entire room.

"Dad, can we go look in some of the other museum rooms while you wait for Mr. Howard and Mr. O'Brien?" Veronica asks, as Alex nods in agreement.

"Sure, but be back here in ten minutes,"

Dad says, keeping his eye on the display case.

"Okay." The twins quickly run off.

Dad walks over to the case where we found the necklace and removes the glass cover from the base. Why is he looking there? The necklace was in the drawer at the bottom. He moves his hands all around the top edge of the base and suddenly stops.

I think I'll give up my search and watch Dad.

He tilts the display case.

"Hank! What are you doing?" Mr. Howard says as he re-enters the room.

"Take a look, John."

Mr. Howard puts a large book on a chair and carefully studies the case.

"What am I looking for?" Mr. Howard asks after examining the entire top of the display case.

"Let me look!" Chief O'Brien inserts, as he marches toward the case.

Mr. Howard moves aside. The chief is more thorough in his examination, but also asks, "What am I supposed to see?"

Dad once again holds the display case. He points to something I can't see.

"Hank, I must be either losing my eyesight, or my mind," the chief snorts.

"The switch for the alarm on the case has been altered, making it possible to prevent the signal from sounding. And by the looks of it, whoever did the work knew what they were doing."

"Do you think that the insurance people are responsible?" Mr. Howard asks with concern.

"It certainly appears that way," Dad replies. "Do you have the card?"

"Over there, Hank." Mr. Howard's hand quivers as he points. "Please give me the book and I'll get it for you."

Dad picks up the big black book and hands it to Mr. Howard, who turns several pages and removes a small white card. He passes the card to Dad.

Dad holds it up to the light. "I can't tell anything until I get the card from Jerry."

I put my paws on Dad's knee to see.

"Get down, Upton."

Mr. O'Brien and the twins join us.

"Here's a card of a guy from the insurance company who I met last month."

Jerry O'Brien hands the printed business card to Dad, who immediately holds it up to the light. He takes the card Mr. Howard gave him and puts it next to the other card.

"And...?" the chief asks after a few seconds, watching Dad compare the cards.

"Can't tell. They look very similar," Dad says. "But that doesn't really mean a thing. If the necklace is a fake, a good fake, I assume the card could be a good fake also."

I hope I don't get too dizzy watching Dad and the chief talk, but I'm dying to know what happens, even if I can't see a thing.

"Now what do you suggest?" The chief sounds impatient. "Walter Jacobi won't be done for a while. Shouldn't we contact the Van Camps?"

"It's Saturday, and the insurance company

offices will most likely be closed, so we can't find out if..." Dad looks at the card, "Mr. Freeman is an employee or an imposter until Monday morning."

"Dad, maybe Mr. Freeman has a cell phone and you could call him today," Alex suggests.

Everyone stops talking.

Dad looks at the card in his hand. "Chief, can I use your cell phone?"

"Sure. Why?"

"Because my brilliant son has just given us the solution to our immediate problem and I need your caller-ID to come up on his phone."

"Hank, please be more specific," Mr. Howard says.

"Mr. Freeman's card lists a cell number. I simply overlooked that fact when I compared the card with the other, because they both have cell numbers. Call the number and we will either get Mr. Freeman, in which case he works for the insurance company. Or the cell number is also phony... just like the necklace."

This all makes perfect sense to me. Let's call, and hurry.

Dad dials the number. It rings and rings. Finally Dad says, "Chief, what's the number of your phone?"

"671-555-0417. Why?"

"I've got his voice mail. Wait." He pauses to listen to the instructions and then says: "Hi. This is Hank Charles. Please give me a call as soon as possible at 671-555-0417. It concerns the Van Camp necklace. I am a trustee of the museum. Thanks."

"What happened?" the twins chime.

"He is either on the phone or the phone is not turned on, but the message said, 'Hi, this is John Freeman of Consolidated Insurance, please leave a message and I'll get back to you as soon as I can.' So, I asked him to call the chief's phone."

"Sounds like he's for real. But does that help us?" the chief wonders.

Dad stares at Chief O'Brien. "The insurance guys who were here three days ago looked at both the security system and the necklace. Maybe we can find out if the genuine Van Camp necklace was ever really on display."

"Are you implying that the museum never had the authentic necklace in the first place?"

I feel really bad for Mr. Howard. I'd hate to be in his shoes. Wait a minute! I don't wear shoes!

"Or it's possible that the real necklace was later exchanged with the imitation," Jerry O'Brien says.

"But why steal, or attempt to steal a fake?" the chief joins in.

This is all very complicated.

Suddenly the chief's cell phone rings. Dad hands it back to him.

"Chief O'Brien speaking," he announces loudly. "Yes, here he is." He hands the phone back to Dad.

"It's John Freeman, returning your call."

CHAPTER TEN
A Break for Hot Chocolate

"Mr. Freeman? Hank Charles," Dad says into the phone. "Thanks for calling back so quickly. A problem has arisen concerning the Van Camp necklace, and I'm sorry to be asking this on a Saturday, but do you have a few minutes you can spare to meet me at the museum?"

Everyone closes in on Dad, trying to hear Mr. Freeman's voice.

"It is rather important," Dad continues. "I'm presently meeting at the museum with John

Howard, Jerry O'Brien, and Chief of Police Charlie O'Brien. Yes, that will be great. See you then."

By now everyone is within a few feet of where Dad is standing...even me.

"Mr. Freeman is on his way over. He thinks it will take about half an hour. He doesn't have his file at home, but he remembers the necklace. The other man from the insurance company, the one who was appraising the necklace, doesn't live around here, but Mr. Freeman said he'll try and reach him at home. He recalls that the appraiser said the necklace was in excellent condition for a piece of its age, and there is no question in Mr. Freeman's mind that the piece of jewelry was authentic when he was here. In any event, he'll have an investigator from the insurance company here on Monday."

"That was a brilliant idea you two had."

Mr. Howard seems pleased for the first time today.

Alex gives Veronica a look and says, "Just because we're twins, it doesn't mean you should take credit when it was my idea."

"Oh, be quiet, Alex. I would have come up with the same thing anyway," Veronica replies.

"Right!"

Alex is correct. Veronica does sometimes try and make people think something is her idea when it's really Alex's. On the other hand, Alex does the same thing to Veronica. Maybe because they're twins, they actually get the same idea at the same time. That is a scary thought.

Since we have a half an hour to wait for Mr.

Freeman to arrive, I will continue exploring.

"Hey, kids, we've got a little time before Mr. Freeman gets here, how about a hot chocolate? And we can take Upton for a walk."

Now that is a simply brilliant idea. Where is my leash?

"Jerry, let's go get something to eat and drink." The chief turns to his brother, who nods in agreement. "John, do you want anything?"

"Yes, thanks Chief. I really could use a black coffee," Mr. Howard says.

"Donut? Bagel?" the chief asks.

"No, thanks, I've got to watch the waistline."

Maybe the O'Brien brothers should take the hint from Mr. Howard and skip the donuts.

"Okay, see you in thirty minutes."

Dad hooks on my leash, which I retrieved from the floor where it had been dropped. Let's get this show on the road.

I hadn't realized how much I needed to visit a tree or two. I don't care about fire hydrants. That is something people like to believe dogs like, but is completely wrong. Most dogs couldn't care less about fire hydrants. We start to walk down the street back toward my favorite coffee shop. Dogs do have favorite coffee shops though. The kind with the outdoor tables where I can sit and beg for some pastry, or maybe a bit of sandwich. Well, not really beg, more like...request.

"Who wants something to eat?" Dad asks the twins.

Dad also seems in a lot better mood after finding out the men from the insurance company

59

are real and not fake. I bet he wishes the same could be said of the Van Camp necklace. There are a lot of questions still unanswered. For example, is the necklace we found genuine? Probably not. If the necklace in the case was the original when the insurance men looked at it, where is it now? And who took it and replaced it with the copy? Wow, Dad has his work cut out for him. This is not going to be easy.

"Can we each have a donut?" Veronica asks.

"Let me see, as I recall, each of you was eating a donut when I came downstairs this morning. Then you both devoured several pieces of French toast. Now, you want another donut?"

The twins look at the floor.

"I don't think so. How about some soup?" Dad asks.

"Pizza?" Alex adds.

"We don't have the time. Later, I promise."

"Just hot chocolate will be fine for now," Veronica announces cheerfully.

Fortunately, the weather is getting warmer and we can sit outside without freezing. The kids sip their hot chocolate while Dad drinks a cappuccino, which is like coffee, but it has this white foamy stuff on top. Nothing for me. Gee, thanks guys.

On the way back to the museum, no one speaks. I wonder if everyone is thinking about the missing necklace. It's like a giant puzzle. We need to find out who, why, and where. Whether the Van Camp necklace was exchanged for the fake necklace before or during the museum party last night is very important in trying to find out who took it. How the necklace was stolen is the last thing we need to find out, I think. What confuses me most is that if someone traded the real one for the fake, why try to hide the fake? Maybe one person exchanged the two necklaces and another person tried to hide the copy, thinking it was the original. This is getting very confusing. I am sure that is why everyone is so quiet. We are all deep in thought.

When we arrive back at the museum, I immediately notice a huge car. It's like Dad's Jeep, only bigger...a lot bigger.

"Dad, Dad, can we get a Hummer like that?" The kids point at the gigantic vehicle in the driveway, while I try to figure out why anyone would want such a big car. For one thing, I couldn't ever stick my face out the window—it's too high up.

"No, children. No way. It wouldn't even fit in the driveway." Dad shakes his head and smiles. I am so glad he has good taste in selecting cars.

As we enter the museum, Mr. Howard meets us. He is standing next to a small bald man with glasses, wearing a dark blue jacket with the word *Hummer* on the back. I can't believe a man that small is driving a car that big.

"Hank, I'd like you to meet John Freeman. He was one of the two men from the insurance company who inspected the exhibit the other day."

Mr. Freeman extends his hand to Dad. "Hi. Everyone calls me Jack."

"Thanks for dropping everything on such short notice, and on a Saturday."

"No big deal. The only thing I had planned for today was to wash the wheels."

I think Mr. Freeman is talking about washing his entire car, since it doesn't make any sense to wash only the wheels. You might as well wash the whole thing. People talk so funny sometimes.

"Hank, I've shown Mr. Freeman around and generally filled him in on what we've found out so far," Mr. Howard says. "He wasn't able to reach Mr. Singleton, who appraised the necklace, but left a message with his wife to have him call either Mr. Freeman's cell phone or here at the museum."

"I've had a chance to look at the overall security system, and I'm certain it hasn't been tampered with or set off. However, I can confirm that the contact on the case was altered, which took the display case off the alarm system," Mr. Freeman explains.

"Let me understand you. No one entered the museum while the alarm was on, but the top of the case could have been lifted up at any time while there was someone in the museum?" Dad asks.

Mr. Freeman nods. "Exactly."

"The only time the room was open to the public was during the event last night." Mr. Howard looks worried again.

"What about people who help set up the show?" Dad asks.

"The entire exhibit was set up before the necklace was put in the case," Mr. Howard says.

"And Mr. Freeman and Mr. Singleton

viewed the necklace in the case, correct?" Dad seems to be going somewhere with his questions, and I think I understand.

"Yes. We examined the necklace last Thursday at about ten in the morning, after the exhibit had been set up."

Dad listens carefully to Mr. Freeman.

"So the swap was made sometime after ten on Thursday and before midnight last night," Dad says.

"Dad? When was the pretend necklace taken out of the case?" Veronica asks.

"To whom do these children belong?" Mr. Freeman asks.

"Sorry, Jack. This is my daughter, Veronica and my son, Alex."

Both twins extend their hands to shake Mr. Freeman's.

"And this is Upton. He found the imitation necklace."

Thank you, Dad. How considerate of him to introduce me. Mr. Freeman bends down and offers to shake my paw.

I return the favor because I know how to be polite. Dad taught me that when I was much younger.

CHAPTER ELEVEN
Who Stole the Necklace?

"I don't want to rain on anyone's parade, but are we really any closer now than we were a couple of hours ago?"

The chief makes it sound as if we are not doing anything.

"Chief, let's take a close look at what we've actually accomplished in a couple of hours," Dad says. "We've recovered a necklace, although it appears to be a copy. We know that the real necklace was here two days ago. We know that nobody broke into the museum. And we know that the insurance policy will pay millions to the Van Camps. I consider that progress."

Once again, everyone crowds around Dad. It's like that when he talks. People really listen. He is so smart.

"And we know some other things, too. Like somebody changed the real necklace with the copy," Alex adds.

"That someone ruined the alarm part of the display case," Veronica says.

"And we know that someone tried to hide the phony necklace," Mr. Howard says.

"Excellent. Anyone else?" Dad asks.

"Well," Jerry O'Brien begins, "we know that the insurance people who came to the museum are real."

"There was a possibility that whoever visited the museum the other day didn't work for the insurance company but were actually the thieves," the chief says, jumping into the discussion.

Mr. Freeman shakes his head. "And it's too much like the movies."

"Okay," Dad continues. "Let's focus on the remaining questions. Other than the Van Camps, who might want to steal the necklace?" Dad looks around the room for someone to answer.

I wish I could raise my hand and ask a basic question.

"Which necklace?" Thank you, Alex, for hearing my thoughts.

"That is a very good question, young man,"

Mr. Howard offers.

Hey, it was my idea. Oh well.

"I think that whoever exchanged the genuine necklace with the counterfeit is a different person from whoever took the imitation necklace and hid it in the bottom drawer."

Chief O'Brien walks back and forth as he speaks, with his hands behind his back. He looks kind of silly. He walks about three steps, stops, turns around, and then walks back three steps. Maybe he thinks better that way.

I've got a good idea. No...a great idea. I just hope someone else thinks about it and quickly, because what we do next could be a mistake. Dad looks at me, and I start to wag my tail. "What is it, Upton? You are on to something, aren't you?"

"I agree that we do have a lot of information," Chief O'Brien says, and finally stops pacing. "But it suggests that we are now looking for different suspects, one for taking the original necklace and substituting the fake necklace, and one for the hiding the fake, probably so that he or she could steal it later."

"Are we?" Dad asks.

Keep talking, Dad. I think I know where you are heading.

"What if whoever hid the pretend necklace was trying to take our attention away from the real robbery?" Dad says.

You're almost there, Dad, but not quite.

"If the same person took the real necklace and replaced it with the fake one and then hid the fake. Hold on! Since no one knew the necklaces had been switched, everyone would think the fake was real and—"

"And that someone would not only have the original necklace but—" the chief interrupts Dad.

"A cool multi-million-dollar settlement as well," Jerry O'Brien interrupts his brother.

"If the fake was found, even assuming it to be real, there would be no insurance."

Dad is getting warmer. Everyone is interrupting everyone else but they are almost at the answer of *who*, which means we don't really have to get to *why* and *how* the real necklace was stolen.

Suddenly Dad's cell phone rings. Frantically he searches his pockets. Finally he answers, "Hello." Dad's face changes expressions several times during his conversation. He hangs up and finds everyone has closed in around him.

"It was Mother," he says to the twins. The group starts to walk away. "She decided to get her nails done, and guess who sat down next to her? Mrs. Van Camp."

When he says her name, everyone suddenly turns. "Apparently, Mrs. Van Camp broke several nails and needed them fixed immediately," he says.

"So?" Chief O'Brien shakes his head and resumes walking away.

"When the pictures were being taken of Mrs. Van Camp, her nails were perfect. I can even remember the photographer commenting on the bright red color," Mr. Howard observes.

"So she broke them this morning. Big deal."

"Or last night...after the party."

Good job Alex.

"What if I told you Chief, that my wife overheard Mrs. Van Camp saying that the necklace is like a family curse, not a blessing, and that she wishes she could hock it and be rid of the thing forever?"

"Dad, what does hock mean?" Veronica

asks.

"Oh, sorry, sweetie, it means kind of like sell."

"So Mom heard Mrs. Van Camp say she wants to sell the necklace?" Alex adds.

"Basically," Dad replies.

"Why don't you just call Mrs. Van Camp and ask her to come over here?" Veronica suggests. "Then we can ask her."

"That's actually a pretty good idea, Veronica, but maybe we should ask Mr. Van Camp instead," Dad says. "Chief?"

"Why not?" Chief O'Brien says. "Hank, if you make the call, it's not official and might not raise his suspicion. He can refuse, or he can come over and tell us his side of the story. Good thinking, little lady. Real good thinking."

The chief smiles.

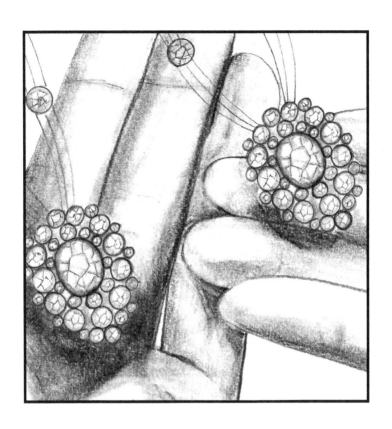

CHAPTER TWELVE
Many Necklaces, Many Thieves?

"Hank, do you have a plan?" Mr. Howard asks with continued concern. "The Van Camps are very important contributors to the museum, and I would hate to alienate them and their friends. You know how difficult it is to get donations."

"Where are you going with this?" the chief asks.

"We've been here all morning so a few more minutes won't make any difference," Dad states.

Everyone nods.

"What question do we need to answer next?" The chief seems confused.

"When was the necklace stolen?" Jerry O'Brien joins the discussion.

"Dad, which necklace are we talking about?" Veronica asks proudly.

"Now there's the best question I've heard so far," Dad says. "If we can find out whether there are two thieves or only one thief who stole the necklace, replaced it with a fake one, and then hid the fake, the rest of the puzzle will be quickly solved."

"How so?" Mr. Howard asks.

"Think about it, John. If there are two thieves, the first thief had a plan which included a lot of advance preparation, while the second thief may simply have seized the moment, not realizing that he or she was stealing a fake—which, personally, I doubt. However, if there is only one thief, he or she stole the imitation necklace only to disguise the previous theft of the real necklace...to throw us off the track. I don't think the imitation necklace was hidden, expecting us to find it because that defeats the motive."

"What motive?" the chief shouts.

"For insurance money...and to keep the original necklace," Dad continues.

"If Upton hadn't found the lost stone, we might not have suspected that it wasn't real!" Alex says.

Thank you, Alex. I very much appreciate the compliment.

"Excellent," Dad continues. "The necklace

we found was a very good copy of the original. It took skill, time, and money to make it. Whoever made the second necklace, or had it made, had access to the real necklace, in order to make sure they looked alike. But it was a back-up."

Sounds like he's got another idea, and I think I know what it is.

"What you're saying, Hank, makes sense and clearly points to the Van Camps," Jerry O'Brien says. "Based on the information they gave me when the museum applied for insurance the necklace had never been publicly exhibited before. They were the only ones who could have had the copy made."

"You're making a case that I should bring them both to the station for questioning," the chief says.

"Possibly, but I propose an easier approach," Dad says. "They may have a logical explanation for the copy, and we don't want to go around accusing someone without some more evidence."

"We have plenty of evidence," the chief says. "It's their necklace and they had it. So only they could make a copy, and they would get the insurance money. I think they should be questioned immediately."

"So do I, Chief, but in a way that might not arouse their suspicion. Let me suggest another possibility. The Van Camps might have had the necklace cleaned or repaired, or even appraised, which would have given someone else the opportunity to have a copy made. That person could be the thief, and the insurance wasn't a consideration because it was planned that no one would know there had been an exchange."

"Whatever, I want to talk with the Van Camps...now," the chief says

"Let me suggest something." Mr. Freeman walks toward the display case. "It has been my experience that the simplest plan is usually the most successful. The more complicated, the more likely something will go wrong. The existence of the fake necklace may have three explanations: to use it as a cover-up for the theft, to use it as a decoy and finally to be sure that the real necklace is never stolen."

"That's not simple. That's confusing," Alex says.

"I'm sorry. People will often make a copy of

an expensive piece of jewelry. They will wear the imitation, especially if it is a quality reproduction, out to parties, and keep the original in the bank vault."

"What's the point of owning something and not wearing it?" Veronica asks.

"Good question and one I really can't answer. People own expensive antique cars and don't drive them. It's the same thing. The original jewelry or car is so expensive, people are afraid of it being stolen or damaged."

I can tell Veronica is lost in thought. She looks at Mr. Freeman. "What you're saying is that grown-ups own things just to own things...not to wear, play with, drive or enjoy...simply to own. It doesn't make any sense."

"Well, dear, it does, in a way," Dad suggests. "Sometimes it is how people judge other people... by what they own...not who they are. They think that they are what they own. I don't agree with that perception, but I know some people who really feel that way. Although, I don't think most people are really like that."

Since dogs really don't own anything, we are who we are. Maybe people should try harder to be more like us.

"Mr. Jacobi expressed the opinion that the copy would have had to be made from the original," Dad reminds us. "One thing we do know is that the case was opened at least four times."

"Four!" Mr. Howard exclaims.

"Yes, John. At least four times from the time Mr. Freeman and the appraiser were here until this morning. I am pretty sure about the order: once when the copy and the original were exchanged, once when the copy was worn by Mrs. Van Camp for the photo session, once when the necklace was returned to the case after the photographs had been taken, and finally when the copy was put in the bottom drawer. So the alarm on the case must have been disconnected since before the original was removed."

"Well, that settles it." Everyone stares at Veronica as she continues. "One person stole both necklaces."

"Hold on there, young lady," the chief announces. "Unless you have some secret information I haven't heard, there is no possible way I can reach the same conclusion."

His brother nods in agreement.

Good thinking, Veronica. I really think you're on the right track.

CHAPTER THIRTEEN
Veronica Has an Idea

Everyone looks at Veronica, waiting to hear what she'll say. "To...like get to the necklace, the alarm would have to be turned off...right?"

I see the chief nodding his head just a little. I don't think he likes an eleven-year-old girl being the center of attention.

"The sign on the display case even says, DO NOT TOUCH—ALARM WILL SOUND," Veronica continues.

"Brilliant, young lady," says Mr. Freeman.

"Please continue," Dad says.

"The thief broke the alarm so that it wouldn't ring when he or she stole the real necklace and replaced it with the fake. And when the fake was stolen—"

"Actually, hidden so we could find it," Alex interrupts.

"But not so it would be found. It was hidden to be removed later," Veronica continues.

"Wait, I got it." Alex starts to jump up and down. "The thief who changed the real necklace with the fake knew the alarm wasn't working, so unless the first thief and the second thief are the same person how would the thief who hid the fake necklace know it wasn't working?"

"Wait a minute," the chief shouts, "I don't agree. I...I..."

"Think about it. Who would know the alarm for the case wasn't functioning, except for the person who broke it?" Veronica questions.

"The thief himself or an accomplice," Mr. Howard offers.

"Or herself," Alex suggests.

"Hank, between your kids and your dog, I'd be out of a job." The chief grins.

Veronica and Alex smile. Me...I'm proud and wag my tail to show it. A dog treat would be real nice about now.

"Okay, but who is the most likely suspect?" Mr. Freeman looks at the twins.

"Veronica, Alex, any ideas?" Dad asks.
Looking at each other, then at Dad, they say, "the Van Camps".

"Which one?" the chief demands.

The twins shrug. "Mrs. Van Camp broke her nails after the party. Maybe she was trying to open the secret drawer?"

"But you said there was only one thief." The chief isn't smiling anymore.

"Or a thief and an accomplice, like Mr. Howard pointed out," Mr. Freeman jumps in.

"We don't have any real proof. Let's get them down to the station and—" the chief is blustering again.

"Chief, go slow. I thought you agreed to let me talk to Mr. Van Camp."

Dad speaks as softly as the chief speaks loudly.

"That was before your children figured out the one thief or—one thief and a partner theory."

Dad calmly says, "That really doesn't change anything yet. Give me an hour."

"We've got to get them before they leave town," the chief yells. "So what are you going to do in an hour?"

I wonder if by talking real loud a person thinks that what he is saying is more important. I think it just hurts everyone's ears.

"Chief, when I spoke to my wife a little while ago, I told you she said she saw Mrs. Van Camp at the beauty salon. She's not leaving town before her nails are done."

The chief's mouth opens, but nothing comes out. Three cheers for Dad...and Mom.

"One hour!" the chief finally says.

"One hour." Dad smiles.

CHAPTER FOURTEEN
A Plan to Catch a Thief

Dad pulls out his cell phone and starts to call someone. "Quick question, darling," he says into the phone. "Is Mrs. Van Camp still getting her nails done? I'll explain later...perfect...thanks. I love you." Dad hangs up. "Mrs. Van Camp is still at the salon and will be there for..." looking at the chief, "another hour."

"Okay, Hank, your spy network is better than our police force...sometimes." The chief smiles again.

On occasion the chief can be so nice, and then again he can act so mean. Dad isn't paying attention, because he is making another phone call.

"May I speak with Mr. Jacobi?" All eyes turn toward Dad. "Walter? Hank...yeah...could you bring the necklace and the loose stone back to the museum soon? I also need you to play a part in a show we're preparing. We hope it will catch a thief...or two. Great. Half an hour is perfect." He hangs up. "John, do you have the Van Camps' home number?"

"Not only that, Hank, but I've got his cell phone as well. I'll get it." Mr. Howard walks off toward his office.

"Mr. Freeman, you have a role in this play as well, if you are willing...and you too, Jerry."

"I would not miss it for the world," Mr. Freeman exclaims.

"Count me in," Mr. O'Brien adds.

"What about me?" asks the chief.

"Chief, I don't want to hurt your feelings, but I don't want to scare anybody, and I think a police presence might do just that."

"But this is a robbery and I am the police."

"Exactly. I want you here. But I don't want anyone to see you."

"I'm a little too big to stand in a corner or hide in a vent. What do you suggest?"

Dad and I look up at the same time.

"The roof?" the chief asks.

"Yes," Dad replies. "It's perfect. You can see and hear what's going on, and it's a beautiful day."

Mr. Howard rushes in with a piece of paper. "Here, Hank...the Van Camps' phone numbers."

Once again, Dad dials his cell phone. It seems as if it is ringing forever.

"Hello? Mr. Van Camp? I'm Hank Charles, a trustee of the museum. Yes. It was a wonderful event, and thank you for the generous loan of your family's necklace. And it is because of the necklace that I'm calling. Is it possible for you to spare a few minutes and come down to the museum? Yes, of course he's here. Do you want to speak to him? I understand. It'll only take a few minutes, fifteen minutes, tops, sir. Thank you."

Dad hangs up. "John, how can you deal with that man? He is so rude."

The twins instinctively move next to Dad. So do I.

Mr. Howard shakes his head. "I'm sorry, Hank. It's just that the Van Camps have been supporting the museum for years."

"I understand, but..." Dad stops speaking.

Dad decides not to say anything else. Whatever Mr. Van Camp said hurt must have hurt Dad's feelings. Maybe it was how he said it. Being important doesn't give you the right to be inconsiderate. Nothing gives you the right to be inconsiderate.

CHAPTER FIFTEEN
Pizza Break

What perfect timing for a walk. I discover my leash still lying where the twins dropped it earlier. Being polite and considerate, I carry it over to them, who pay absolutely no attention to me whatsoever.

"Dad?" Veronica gently pulls his sleeve. "I'm hungry."

"Me, too," Alex says.

Me too, but I need a walk first. Hello?

"I think we've all earned a lunch break, a

quick lunch break," Dad says. "Walter Jacobi will arrive in twenty minutes."

"And when is Mr. Van Camp expected?" Mr. Freeman asks.

"About forty-five minutes."

Suddenly Mr. Howard's assistant, Chris, comes into the room. "I've taken the liberty of ordering pizza and soft drinks. They'll be here in about ten minutes."

"Wonderful idea. Wonderful," the chief says.

I guess he's getting hungry, too. He doesn't look like he misses too many meals.

"Well, it was Mr. Howard's idea. I've set up a place to eat in the conference room on the second floor."

"Hey, Upton, want to go for a walk?"

Alex finally notices me. It's about time. Yes, please, and as soon as possible.

"Dad, we're going to take Upton out, okay?"

"Sure, just be back in time for pizza." He returns to his conversation with Mr. Freeman.

Trust me Dad, I'm not going to let anyone be late for pizza, especially me.

Alex takes my leash, and out we go. Couple of trees, a stop sign, and we're back, just in time to meet the A-1 Pizza man delivering three extra-large pizzas and a bag of soft drinks. Life is good. Everyone finds a seat in the conference room.

"Plain, pepperoni and mushroom, or veg-gie?" Chris asks.

He takes the orders and places a slice on each plate. Okay, I don't get a plate but I still like...

no, love...pizza. I deliberately meander among the chairs, looking for a handout. No luck. Time for the old sneeze trick. Dad looks down at me and smiles.

"Chris, may I have an extra plate?" Dad starts to cut up some pizza crust.

The twins do the same thing. My favorite part of pizza is the crust. As Dad puts the plate on the floor, Chris places a small bowl of water next to me. Now that's being considerate.

"Got any more?" We all turn as Mr. Jacobi joins us in the conference room. In his hands is a briefcase, which he pats. "Got the necklace, and it is a copy, every last stone is synthetic, man-made. Probably crafted only two or three years ago. And my guess is that it was made in Thailand. Very good workmanship."

Mr. Jacobi grins as he takes his first bite of pepperoni and mushroom pizza. Don't forget to save me the crust.

CHAPTER SIXTEEN
Upton Finds Another Clue

After cleaning up the mess from lunch, we all return to the exhibit room except the chief and Chris, who go to the roof. Dad is really clever. He's got everything figured out. I think even the chief is impressed.

"How much longer until Mr. Van Camp gets here?" Alex asks.

"Just a few minutes more, son," Dad replies.

Since I don't have much to do, I start walking around the exhibits, sniffing here, poking there. What's this? I look around to find Dad, who is talking with Mr. Jacobi and Mr. Freeman. I hate to bother him, but, well, here goes. I yip! Suddenly everyone turns around and stares at me with a "this had better be good" kind of look. I wag my tail and bark again. Dad hustles over.

"Mr. Freeman, please take a look at this." He picks up a small black plastic and metal piece.

"It's the original switch from the display case. Whoever removed it either dropped it by accident or was in a hurry and threw it away. They didn't know we had Super Dog..." Dad looks at me, "on the job."

Veronica leans over and scratches my ear. "Good work, baby dog."

Ugh! I hate being called 'baby dog', but I do like my ear being scratched.

"You are such a smart dog," Alex chimes in. I am overwhelmed. All this praise. Truthfully, I love it.

"Does the switch tell us anything new?" Dad asks Mr. Freeman.

"Yes and no. Basically it looks as though someone exchanged switches, took off the two wires from the original, and replaced it with the new switch, which makes the alarm system think the display case is closed when it is actually open. Consequently, there's no alarm noise."

"Could the switch have been removed without setting off the alarm?" Veronica asks as she walks over to the display case.

"Excellent question. Let me think. The alarm should sound unless the entire system is shut off or—" Mr. Freeman stops talking and rushes toward the case. He removes the top from the case, reaches into his pocket, and takes out a red knife with all sorts of tools attached to it, like a screwdriver and saw. It even has a pair of pliers, which Mr. Freeman uses to pull some wires out of the display case. He pulls and pulls Mr. Free- man stops and holds up the two wires he retrieved. Small pieces of tape are attached to each wire.

"The alarm switch was removed when these wires were taped together. The person who did this, our thief, knows how an alarm system works."

"My, my...what a gathering," a voice booms from the door.

"Mr. Van Camp, thank you for coming." Mr. Howard rushes over to shake his hand.

Dad follows, offering his as well. "Hi, I'm Hank Charles."

"I know who you are. Let's get on with this," Mr. Van Camp growls.

He didn't even shake Dad's hand. I'd like to bite him!

CHAPTER SEVENTEEN
Mr. Van Camp Tells All

Dad just shrugs, as Mr. Van Camp strides past him toward the case.

"Where is the necklace?" Mr. Van Camp demands.

"It's right here," Mr. Jacobi replies, as he opens the black velvet case he is holding.

"Let me explain," Dad says. "Mr. Howard noticed a problem with the necklace when he opened the museum this morning."

Mr. Van Camp doesn't look so good.

"There's a problem? What problem?" he shouts.

"Apparently, while your wife was being photographed with the necklace, a stone fell out. When he noticed it was missing this morning, he called me, and I, in turn, called Mr. O'Brien, the insurance agent, Mr. Freeman, who is a representative of the insurance company, and Mr. Jacobi, whose technical assistance we required and whom I understand you know."

"We have met..." Mr. Van Camp states, nodding in Mr. Jacobi's direction, "in passing. I believe my wife may have had her watch fixed in your store."

Mr. Van Camp has an attitude.

"As luck would have it, I decided to walk over to the museum to see the necklace for myself and offer assistance to Mr. Howard—" Dad says.

"Just get to the point," Mr. Van Camp rudely interrupts.

"Well, I decided to bring my children and our dog with me and to make a long story short—"

"Please do," Mr. Van Camp sounds angry. "Our dog Upton found the missing stone, which must have fallen out of a loose setting. Since the stone has been found, we only need your permission to place it back into the necklace, at the museum's expense, of course."

"You called me down here for that?" Mr. Van Camp takes several steps toward Dad. Now they are about a foot apart.

Dad tries to remain cool. "Well, actually, Mr. Van Camp, the insurance company has decided to cancel the policy, and has insisted the museum remove the piece from the exhibit. We would like to return the necklace to you...now."

Mr. Van Camp looks as though he is going to fall over. "Now? The necklace? You want to return it to me now?"

"Walter says he can reinstall the stone in a couple of minutes," Dad says calmly.

"But...but...what shall I do with it?" Mr. Van Camp sputters.

"You have a safe at your home, don't you?" Mr. Howard suggests. "I'm sure you told me that when you brought the necklace here last week."

"Yes...but—" Suddenly, Mr. Van Camp's cell phone rings. "Hello? Yes dear...very good... I'll be right there." Mr. Van Camp hangs up. He looks around the room.

"I've got to go now... to pick up my wife. Can't be late."

"No problem, sir," Dad says. "My wife is also at the salon, and she'd be pleased to bring Mrs. Van Camp here. The insurance company insists the necklace be returned immediately."

"We'll need you to sign this receipt and a release," Mr. Freeman joins in.

"While you were talking, I put the stone back in. It looks as if one of the hooks holding the stone got snagged on a piece of clothing and bent, allowing the stone to fall from the setting. It's as good as new...or shall I say, as good as old." Mr. Jacobi chuckles at his own joke.

"I really don't have time for this," Mr. Van Camp says nervously. "I'll deal with the necklace on Monday. I really must go." Mr. Van Camp turns and marches across the room. Suddenly, he stops. Standing at the door is the chief.

"Mr. Van Camp," the chief says in a deep and stern-sounding voice. "Isn't there something you've forgotten to tell us?"

Mr. Van Camp's eyes dart from person to person. There is nowhere to go. He sighs deeply, shrugs and lowers his head. "Yes...I guess there is," he says in a resigned voice.

Mr. Van Camp pauses. He looks as small as the twins. "My wife made me do it. All she thinks about is money. No matter how much I give her, she always wants more. We couldn't just sell the necklace. What would our friends say if they knew we needed money? If the necklace had been stolen from our house, you'd do a lot of investigating into our finances, wouldn't you, Chief?"

The chief slowly nods.

"Displaying the necklace at the museum was perfect. No one would ever suspect us if someone stole it while it was on display. And the copy...I never expected you to find it before we got it out of the museum. I just never...ever expected." Mr. Van Camp's body is shaking.

"I think that you should come with me," the Chief says.

Mr. Van Camp does not resist. The chief leads him out. Everyone watches quietly.

"It's been quite a day," Dad finally says, "and I vaguely remember that I promised you kids a treat."

"Milkshakes!" the twins exclaim.

"No way," Dad says. Then he smiles. "Well, okay. I guess you've each earned a milkshake."

What about me? Yip!

"You get a treat, too, Upton."

"Hank, what should we do with the display?" Mr. Howard asks.

"I suggest we put the imitation necklace back into the display case and put a card next to it saying, *Copy of the Van Camp Necklace.*

I've heard Mom say that *diamonds are a girl's best friend.* I wonder if the pretend diamonds in the Van Camp necklace are man's best friend? Wait—I'm supposed to be man's best friend. Yip!

The Adventures of Upton Charles
by D.G. Stern
Illustrated by Deborah Allison

Disappearing Diamonds
Something Fishy
Winter Wonderland
Lost Loot

Other Books by
D.G. Stern & Deborah Allison

The Loneliest Tree

Upton Charles Dog Detective

Something Fishy

By D.G. Stern

Illustrated By Deborah Allison

Upton and the rest of the Charles family are on vacation in a small coastal town in Maine. Along with his new friend, Storm, the dog detective discovers an abandoned boat near Shell Light. Upton puts his nose to work sniffing out clues lead- ing to the secret of the lighthouse. Follow Upton as he gathers evidence and puts together pieces of the puzzle to solve the mystery in *Something Fishy*.

Visit Upton on the web at:

www.uptoncharles.com

CPSIA information can be obtained
at www.ICGtesting.com
Printed in the USA
JSHW020343270322
24271JS00003B/170